# D d

## Duck & Diamond

E e Eagle &
Egg

Ff Frog & Flag

Goat & Gumballs

# Hh

Hippo &
Hats

# Ii

Iguana & Ice Cream

Jj Jaguar & Juice

Kk

Kangaroo
& Kite

# Ll

Lobster &
Lemonade

# Mm

Monkey &
Mustaches

# Nn

Newt & Newspaper

Ostrich &
Oboe

Penguin &
Pizza

Quail & Quartet

Rabbit &
Ruler

Snake &
Sled

# Tt

Turtle &
Teacup

Vulture &
Vacuum

Walrus & Wizards

X-Ray Fish &
Xylophone

# Yy

yak &
yo-yo

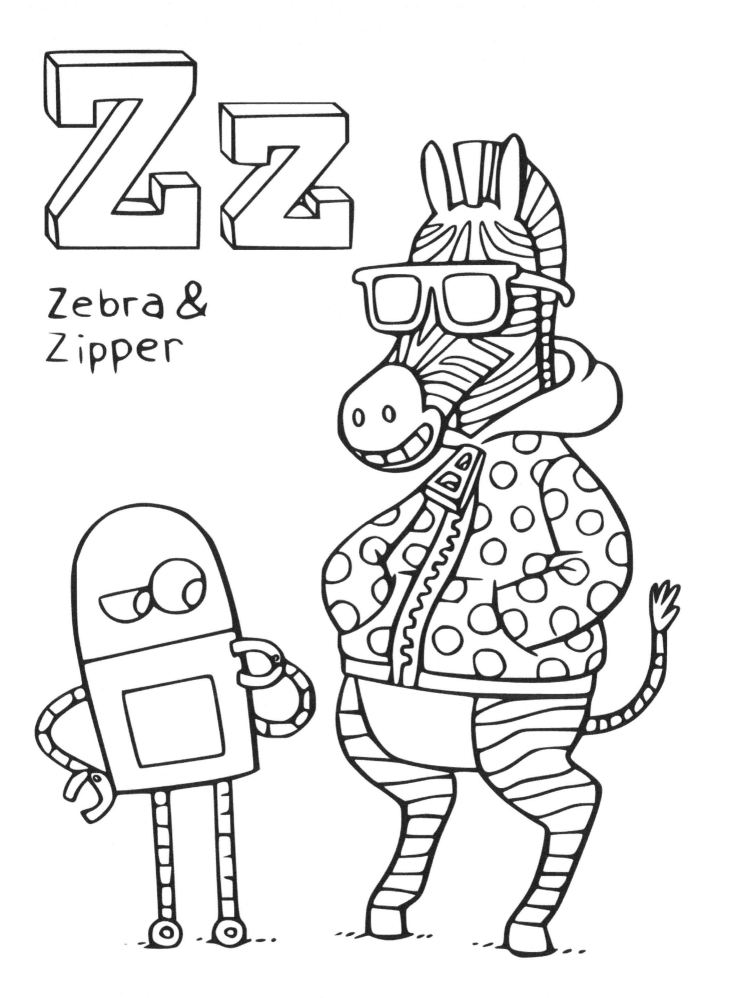

Zz Zz

Zebra &
Zipper

Made in United States
North Haven, CT
12 December 2021

12550737R00033